W9-ACP-483

Sister Rosetta THARPE

BY J. P. MILLER

ILLUSTRATED BY
MARKIA JENAI

Rourke
Educational Media

A Division of
Carson Dellosa Education

BEFORE AND DURING READING ACTIVITIES

Before Reading: *Building Background Knowledge and Vocabulary*

Building background knowledge can help children process new information and build upon what they already know. Before reading a book, it is important to tap into what children already know about the topic. This will help them develop their vocabulary and increase their reading comprehension.

Questions and Activities to Build Background Knowledge:

1. Look at the front cover of the book and read the title. What do you think this book will be about?
2. What do you already know about this topic?
3. Take a book walk and skim the pages. Look at the table of contents, photographs, captions, and bold words. Did these text features give you any information or predictions about what you will read in this book?

Vocabulary: *Vocabulary Is Key to Reading Comprehension*

Use the following directions to prompt a conversation about each word.

- Read the vocabulary words.
- What comes to mind when you see each word?
- What do you think each word means?

Vocabulary Words:
- blues
- contract
- enslaved
- generation
- gospel
- headlined
- orchestra
- promoter

During Reading: *Reading for Meaning and Understanding*

To achieve deep comprehension of a book, children are encouraged to use close reading strategies. During reading, it is important to have children stop and make connections. These connections result in deeper analysis and understanding of a book.

Close Reading a Text

During reading, have children stop and talk about the following:

- Any confusing parts
- Any unknown words
- Text to text, text to self, text to world connections
- The main idea in each chapter or heading

Encourage children to use context clues to determine the meaning of any unknown words. These strategies will help children learn to analyze the text more thoroughly as they read.

When you are finished reading this book, turn to the next-to-last page for **Text-Dependent Questions** and an **Extension Activity**.

TABLE OF CONTENTS

UP TO THE SKY

Have you ever had an idea for doing something in a new and creative way? Did you ever want to share that thing with others? That's how Sister Rosetta Tharpe felt when she played her electric guitar. Her music changed what the world listened to.

Rosetta stepped onto the stage of Carnegie Hall in New York City. Her fingers held the guitar pick tightly. She lifted her head and began singing up to the sky. Incredible sounds came from her guitar. The people watching her were amazed. Rosetta was truly a musical leader.

MAKING HER NAME

Rosetta was six years old when she moved to Chicago, Illinois, with her mother. She spent Sunday mornings at Roberts Temple Church of God in Christ. Those mornings were different from anything she had ever experienced. Jazz musicians from New Orleans blew their horns and scraped washboards. The ones from the Mississippi Delta slid harmonicas across their lips and plucked their guitars. There, she learned how to be a good performer as she sang and played.

Many of the songs that she heard in church were sad. They talked about times when black people were **enslaved** and seeking freedom. Rosetta sang about happier things. When they heard her, people felt like throwing their hands up and celebrating.

Rosetta continued singing and playing guitar in her church as she grew up. She kept doing it when she grew up and married a preacher. But Rosetta's marriage lasted only a few years. Soon, she had a lot of decisions to make. She wanted to keep bringing music to people.

Rosetta packed her guitar and moved to Harlem in New York City. Night clubs were on every street corner. They were looking for new entertainers. Rosetta began performing at the biggest of them all: The Cotton Club.

Rosetta loved God and her church. She loved singing in night clubs too. Some people were upset that she sang church songs in night clubs. She did not let this stop her. Each week, she performed with the Lucky Millinder **Orchestra**. Later, she signed a **contract** with Decca Records. When she performed, she **sang,**

...and picked her guitar,
...and played her heart out!

Famous Names

Rosetta played with very famous musicians. She shared a stage with jazz musician Duke Ellington. She was the star of concerts with the Dixie Hummingbirds.

PRECIOUS MEMORIES

Rosetta was becoming a leader in music. But her hit song "Rock Me" upset her **gospel** fans. Many of them thought she was singing to a man and not to God. Rosetta lost some fans because of it. She worked hard to keep going. Many people loved her new style of music.

A Special Record

Rosetta recorded a song called "Strange Things Happening Every Day" in 1944. It has been called the first rock and roll song.

Rosetta played her guitar and **headlined** concerts. She played the famous Carnegie Hall. She was one of the first musicians to own a special tour bus. She was even asked to play for troops during World War II.

Rosetta worked hard as a musician. She needed to make money. A **promoter** helped her plan a big wedding at Griffith Stadium in Washington, DC. Fans bought tickets to see Rosetta marry for the third time. After the wedding, she performed in front of her biggest crowd ever: 25,000 fans. People had never been to a concert like this!

But the big wedding and concert were not enough for her to stay famous forever. Rosetta retired and started a quiet life. She lived in Pennsylvania with her mother and husband.

One day, Rosetta answered her phone. It was a British promoter. He asked Rosetta to come to the United Kingdom. Rock and roll stars such as Elvis Presley, Buddy Holly, and Johnny Cash were famous now. He wanted people to hear rock and roll from the person who first played it.

When Rosetta was 49 years old, she toured Europe. She was a leader once again. This time, she was sharing rock and roll music with a new **generation**. People around the world had started playing music in new and interesting ways. Although most of them did not know it, Rosetta was a big part of the reason.

Rosetta Tharpe died on October 9, 1973. People called her the Godmother of Rock and Roll. Her name was put into the **Blues** Hall of Fame in 2007. It was put into the Rock and Roll Hall of Fame in 2018. She had always been a leader. Now, people would know about her.

"All this new stuff they call rock 'n roll, why, I've been playing that for years."
—Sister Rosetta Tharpe

TIME LINE

1915 Sister Rosetta Tharpe is born Rosetta Nubin on March 20.

1921 Rosetta moves to Chicago, Illinois, and she starts singing in Church of God in Christ churches.

1930s–1940s Rosetta travels with her mother throughout Chicago and the south. Her mother preaches, and Rosetta sings and plays the guitar.

1936–1937 Rosetta travels to Miami, Florida, with husband. He preaches and Rosetta sings. She is given the chance to sing on local radio.

1938 Rosetta becomes a singer at the Cotton Club in Harlem, New York. She signs a contract with Decca Records.

1944 Rosetta releases the song "Strange Things Happening Every Day." It becomes a number one hit on the Race Chart.

1946 Rosetta meets duet partner and companion Marie Knight. The two travel the country together performing.

1950 Rosetta appears on television for the first time on the Perry Como Supper Club Show.

1958–1960 Rosetta starts her European tour arranged by Chris Barber. She travels to Great Britain, France, Germany, and Scandinavia.

1964–1965 Rosetta makes two guest host appearances on the show *TV Gospel Time*.

1967 Rosetta performs at the Newport Folk Festival in Virginia and tours Europe again.

1973 Rosetta dies on October 9 in Philadelphia, Pennsylvania.

1998 Rosetta is honored by the US Postal Service with a stamp.

2007 Rosetta is put into the Blues Hall of Fame. Gayle Wald publishes *Shout, Sister, Shout!: The Untold Story of Rock and Roll Trailblazer Rosetta Tharpe*, a book about her life.

2008 The Governor of Pennsylvania makes January 11th Rosetta Tharpe Day.

2011 A historical marker is placed in front of Rosetta's Philadelphia home.

2017 Rosetta is put into the Rock and Roll Hall of Fame as an early influencer.

2018 The highway between Rosetta's hometown of Cotton Plant and Brinkly, Arkansas, is renamed the Sister Rosetta Tharpe Highway.

GLOSSARY

blues (blooz): a type of music first sung by African Americans, with songs about difficulties in life and love

contract (KAHN-trakt): a legal agreement between people or companies stating what each of them has agreed to do and any amounts of money involved

enslaved (en-SLAYVD): treated as property by another person

generation (jen-uh-RAY-shun): all the people born around the same time

gospel (GAHS-puhl): music based on the teachings of Jesus

headlined (HED-lined): being the main performer that is advertised the most

orchestra (OR-kuh-struh): an often large group of musicians who play a variety of musical instruments together

promoter (pruh-MOTE-ur): a person who makes the public aware of something or someone

INDEX

TEXT-DEPENDENT QUESTIONS

1. What instrument did Rosetta Tharpe play?

2. Why did some fans not like Rosetta Tharpe's record "Rock Me"?

3. What Harlem, New York, club did Rosetta Tharpe perform in?

4. Where did Rosetta Tharpe tour later in life?

5. What is Rosetta Tharpe known as in rock and roll?

EXTENSION ACTIVITY

Think about what you would like to be famous for doing. You might want to be a famous singer, author, inventor, or something else. Make a poster announcing your world tour. Include the names of all the places you would like to visit on your tour. Think about what you would do at each stop.

ABOUT THE AUTHOR

J. P. Miller is a debut author in children's picture books. She is eager to write stories about little- and well-known African American leaders. She hopes that her stories will augment the classroom experience, educate, and inspire readers. J. P. lives in Metro Atlanta, Georgia, and enjoys playing pickleball and swimming in her spare time.

ABOUT THE ILLUSTRATOR

Markia Jenai was raised in Detroit during rough times, but she found adventure through art and storytelling. She grew up listening to old stories of her family members, which gave her an interest in history. Drawing was her way of exploring the world through imagination.

© 2021 Rourke Educational Media

All rights reserved. No part of this book may be reproduced or utilized in any form or by any means, electronic or mechanical including photocopying, recording, or by any information storage and retrieval system without permission in writing from the publisher.

www.rourkeeducationalmedia.com

Quote source: Wilcox, Desmond. "They Call Her 'Holy Roller': Rosetta Flies in to Rock." *Daily Mirror*, November 22, 1957.

Edited by: Tracie Santos
Illustrations by: Markia Jenai
Cover and interior layout by: Rhea Magaro-Wallace

Library of Congress PCN Data

Sister Rosetta Tharpe / J. P. Miller
(Leaders Like Us)
ISBN 978-1-73163-804-5 (hard cover)
ISBN 978-1-73163-881-6 (soft cover)
ISBN 978-1-73163-958-5 (e-Book)
ISBN 978-1-73164-035-2 (ePub)
Library of Congress Control Number: 2020930199

Rourke Educational Media
Printed in the United States of America
01-1942011937